Pearla

and her
Unpredictably
Perfect Day

A story about how a sprinkling of
mistakes can be a recipe for success

Rochel Lieberman

Illustrated by Lloyd Jones

Jessica Kingsley Publishers
London and Philadelphia

First published in 2017
by Jessica Kingsley Publishers
73 Collier Street
London N1 9BE, UK
and
400 Market Street, Suite 400
Philadelphia, PA 19106, USA

www.jkp.com

Copyright © Rochel Lieberman 2017
Illustrations copyright © Lloyd Jones 2017

Library of Congress Cataloging in Publication Data
A CIP catalog record for this book is available from the Library of Congress

British Library Cataloguing in Publication Data
A CIP catalogue record for this book is available from the British Library

ISBN 978 1 78592 734 8
eISBN 978 1 78450 429 8

Printed and bound in China

To Rashi OBM, you actively sought the perfect in everyone

Every Sunday Pearla's favorite thing to do is to help her dad in his bakery, Knead It! She loves it more than playing checkers or jumping on her pogo stick.

Pearla is only 10, but she is able to bake perfect cookies and cupcakes like a professional baker. Her delicious round cookies with perfect pointy chocolate chips and tall fluffy cupcakes with perfect wiggly white cream are known far and wide.

Each Sunday, just about everyone in Sunshine City comes to buy Pearla's goodies. People even drive from far away to buy her perfect baked goods.

Pearla feels proud that everyone loves her cookies and cupcakes.

It's Sunday morning! Pearla jumps out of bed, precisely picks out her perfect baking clothes and pointy baker hat, and scrambles down the stairs.

She wants to start baking her perfect cookies and cupcakes right away.

She skips all the way down the block to Knead It!

Pearla gathers all the ingredients and lines them up with precision on the counter: flour, eggs, vanilla, butter, and salt.

She picks out her perfect mixing bowl, the one with pink and purple pansies. She begins mixing the ingredients all together in their perfect order.

As she mixes she's thinking about all the people who will come today to eat her cookies and cupcakes.

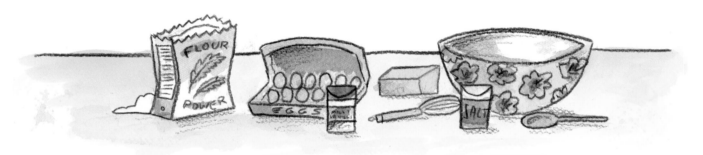

First, she mixes the batter to make her perfectly round cookies.

Next, she uses strong and fast hands to whip her tall fluffy cupcakes.

Into the oven they go!

Oh no
oh no
oh no!

Pearla realizes she forgot to add the baking powder to the cookies and cupcakes. How could she do something so imperfect? But it's too late, the cookies and cupcakes are already beginning to bake.

Pearla starts to feel nervous. She made a mistake, and this is just not okay in Pearla's perfect world.

She doesn't know what to do. Pearla paces back and forth and bites her lip. She mutters softly, "Blllllega Blllllega."

Pearla stands up tall, and takes a deep breath.
She smiles and thinks,

"I'm a person.
People are not perfect.
I did my best.

I know
I will be
helped
with
the rest."

Ding! The timer on the oven goes off. Pearla opens the oven door and peeks inside. She sees that her round circle cookies have come out like triangles and her tall fluffy cupcakes are flat like squares.

"Oh no!" Pearla exclaims. "My cookies and cupcakes are ruined! These are not perfect." She says to herself in a teeny tiny voice,

"Who will want them?"

Pearla plops down to the floor,
and begins twisting her hair
around her finger.
Suddenly, she feels hopeful.

She jumps up and says,

"I have a
plan!

I'm going to sell these imperfect
cookies and cupcakes."

Pearla grabs a thick black marker and writes **"IMPERFECT"** on a large white sign. She places the sign near the triangle cookies and the square cupcakes. She will tell the customers that they can pay less money for these imperfect items.

It's the perfect plan!

Just then, the door creaks open and the Pertraplinski family comes in. Mr. and Mrs. Pertraplinski, along with their dog, are always the first customers and they always, always, always wear triangle shirts, bags, and earrings. Mrs. Pertraplinski even wears triangle-shaped eyeglasses.

Pearla bites her lip and scrunches her eyes shut tight. She's feeling nervous and is just sure the Pertraplinskis will be disappointed to find the imperfect cookies.

Mrs. Pertraplinski walks over to the counter, looks at the cookies and jumps up and down gleefully. "Today is our lucky day!" she shouts out. "This is perfect! We love triangles! We never saw triangle chocolate chip cookies before. These may have a sign that says **IMPERFECT**, but they are perfect for us."

Mrs. Pertraplinski buys two boxes of triangle cookies.

Pearla scratches her head and crinkles her nose. She is very surprised. As she waves goodbye to the Pertraplinskis, she stands behind her imperfect cookies and cupcakes with a big smile on her face.

Up until today, Pearla always thought that making mistakes was not okay.
　　But now she realizes that what is imperfect for one person might be perfect for another.

Pearla turns to see Mrs. Peggyopal and her daughter Darla, both wearing curved oval sunglasses and matching sundresses, enter the store. They drove up all the way from the other side of the river.

Mrs. Peggyopal and Darla are famous for never ever buying anything but Pearla's tall fluffy cupcakes with perfect wiggly white cream. In fact, they even have a taster to test each one.

Mrs. Peggyopal and Darla glare at the imperfect cupcakes. Darla says, "I only eat tall cupcakes with perfectly wiggly white cream. I guess we will just have to buy our cupcakes somewhere else!"

Darla and her mother breathe a heavy sigh and turn their noses up as they leave the store. There are no perfect cupcakes to take home with them today.

Pearla's cheeks grow red.
Her hands begin to feel hot
and sweaty. She feels
embarrassed and sad.

Finally, she takes a long,
deep breath and tells herself,

"I did my best and feel so
thankful for the rest."

Suddenly, Sammy Konstalay, who is on his
way to practice with the Sunshine Swim
Team, rides his scooter into the bakery.

He wears a square helmet, a square watch,
and square shoes, and carries a perfectly
square backpack.

Sammy Konstalay walks over to the counter and gives Pearla a high five. He spies the cupcakes and his eyes get big and square. "Pearla! This is perfect! I love squares! I've never seen square flat cupcakes before. These may have a sign that says **IMPERFECT**, but they are perfect for me."

Sammy Konstalay buys two square flat cupcakes and leaves the bakery with a huge grin on his face.

By now Pearla is feeling even more surprised. She didn't think that anyone would like imperfect flat cupcakes over her perfectly tall ones. She can't believe what has happened.

"Maybe," she thinks, "it's okay when everything doesn't go as perfectly as I think it should. Maybe, just maybe, it's okay to make mistakes."

Soon there is a long line of the Pertraplinskis' sisters, brothers, and neighbors who want to buy their own boxes of imperfect triangle cookies.

Sammy even comes back with children from the Sunshine Swim Team to buy the imperfect square cupcakes.

Pearla stands behind the counter with her mouth wide open. She thinks, "I did my best and feel so thankful for the rest."

By the end of the day there was not even one imperfect cookie or cupcake left in Knead It!

Today Pearla learned an important lesson that she will never forget: Sometimes things don't go perfectly. By staying calm, we might see that imperfect changes can turn into **perfectly perfect plans!**

The End

A Note from the Author

Sometimes (often!) it's humbling to be a writer. I know it's that way for me. We wordsmiths spend endless hours using our very best planning, organizing, visioning, and writing skills, trying to craft the perfect turn of a phrase and the perfect beginning and ending to our stories, and describe our characters on paper as perfectly and vividly as we envision them in our heads. We produce our perfect manuscript and then off it goes to a good editor. All of a sudden we are faced with the imperfections in our previously thought to be carefully perfected work. Despair and anxiety hits; all that red pen! Insecurity strikes. Oh no! Will we ever write again? But then, if we take a deep breath and think about what's before us, if we can accept this as one stop on a longer, larger journey, we can start seeing little rays of light. Hmmm…this word fits better; this sentence sounds stronger; this paragraph really can be deleted. Could it be that what we thought to be so imperfect just minutes ago actually can become more perfect in the end? Dealing with our imperfections is a never-ending situation we all face. How we learn to deal with it can dramatically affect how we come to feel about our lives, and ourselves.

The character of Pearla arose from my many joyful and zany experiences as a writer, as a mom raising my children, and from my years as a speech-language therapist providing services to a wide range of children and adults. Through it all, I observed the growth and powerful learning that clients achieved when they courageously challenged their core beliefs on failure, perfection, and fear of daily challenges. All of us, children, adults, and caregivers alike, are on a journey with many bumps and twists on the surprising road of life. Some of us naturally adapt more easily and can "ride" along without getting too off track. Others, like Pearla, find it more difficult to deal with all the little imperfections, mistakes, and inconveniences that are part of our everyday lives. The store is out of our favorite flavor of ice cream, we have to sit in traffic, or we spill coffee on our shirt right before we have to leave for work and that makes us late. Learning to accept these impossible-to-avoid changes is an important part of our development and can prepare us for challenges that have far greater implications. As one client once said to me, "I am good even though I am not perfect." There is wisdom in those words.

In particular, for children with anxiety, autism spectrum disorder (ASD), ADHD, learning disabilities and/or social learning challenges, life's imperfections can seem devastating. Small problems and unexpected changes can feel monumental. These challenges often bring with them a feeling of confused helplessness, frozen fear, or endless worry, creating an inability to think clearly to figure out a logical solution for even a small problem. Often these feelings can trigger deep shame, with children feeling "less than" for not being able to manage the stressor. Frequently, children and adults can carry these painful feelings, along with the ever elusive search for perfection and order, throughout their life's journey.

Research supports the benefits of stories to build social skills in children with ASD and social challenges, and the calming effects of labeling an emotion, as is done in this story. Yet, this learning is for all children, not just those who struggle or are labeled with a disability. Any adult who has ventured into the land of storytelling with children knows how widespread the benefits can be. Stories let readers connect with people having similar challenges in a non-threatening way. They open the door to on-the-spot questions and sometimes even deeper conversations about the way life works, even when it's not working out well. It is my hope that by reading this book with the children in your life, you can reflect on the story and learn to recognize the triggers that cause Pearla distress. Then, you can have a purposeful conversation to relate these, as applicable, to your own children's, students', or clients' obstacles. And don't worry at all about being perfect in doing so. As Pearla teaches us, sometimes the imperfections lead to utterly perfect outcomes! Some discussion questions are included on the next page to help you engage the children in your life with the story.

Embracing the unknown aspects of life's experiences is important for our emotional health and intelligence. Pearla and her experiences in the bakery show that mistakes are part of the process of life, and that being comfortable with them is more important than being perfect.

Let Pearla guide you and the children in your life toward the path of becoming comfortable with mistakes and the imperfect messiness of our lives. I hope you learn from Pearla. I know I have.

Warmly,
Rochel Lieberman

About the Author

Rochel Lieberman, M.A., CCC-SLP, is a Speech-Language Pathologist, an instructor of language development, and the founder of Ariber Speech, who helps people find their perfect words. Rochel provides workshops at the national, state, and local levels and works with professionals to communicate with the "sound of success." She is currently pursuing a Ph.D. in Communication Sciences and Disorders. Her research interests include social-emotional literacy and stress in language development.

Discussion Questions

Pearla's journey of accepting her mistakes and embracing imperfection is reflective in each one of us. Children who struggle with social delays will benefit greatly when the adult combines reading this inspiring story with using the suggested questions on the opposite page. A discussion can follow about the various coping strategies and tools Pearla has to offer to each individual child's life.

When children get bent out of shape from changes or bumps in their daily routine, you can encourage them to speak up and relate their own story. As the caring adult, you can help them label their emotions (look for the colored information in the story), and then you can talk about everyday situations where they may be feeling or experiencing those emotions. Be sure to help children understand that while the emotions they feel are theirs, to be respected and felt, the expression of those emotions (the behaviors they show) are a different matter. Use Pearla as an example. When Pearla was faced with her imperfect cookies and cupcakes, something that made her upset and nervous, she remained calm and used her flexible thinking to figure out what to do with her baked goods. What if she had been yelling or stomping her feet or having a tantrum in front of the customers instead? They probably would have reacted differently and maybe not even considered buying anything from Pearla. This is a perfect way to talk to children about emotions and different sizes of problems (small, medium, or big) and explain that when we're around other people, it's a hidden social rule that the size of our reaction should match the size of the problem. Helpful resources to extend learning about emotions and emotion regulation are available: various Social Thinking materials by Michelle Garcia Winner, *The Incredible 5-Point Scale* by Kari Dunn Buron and Mitzi Curtis, *The Zones of Regulation* by Leah Kuypers, and *Starving the Anxiety Gremlin* by Kate Collins-Donnelly.

If you expect to be going to a challenging place, with expected tension or changes of schedule, you can better prepare your child by using words to role play the situation and discuss which behaviors are best suited to deal with the expected encounter. From my experience, these conversations are best had either before or after an event, when the child is not in direct contact with the stressor. Remember, repairs are done after the rainstorm. In the middle of a challenging event, whisper words of encouragement and praise to your child. The longer talks, references to Pearla, and conversational questions (such as those that follow) can be saved for dry, sunny days.

I wish you and the children in your life the ability to embrace all that life has to offer, and the foresight to see that it is precisely the little imperfections of our days that contribute to the perfection of it all.

Suggested Questions

After you've read this book with your child, engage in a conversation about making mistakes in general and the thoughts and feelings associated with doing so. Explore this with the child in a casual, rather than "teaching," mode. Use your own life experiences or situations other family members have encountered as examples, so your child is reminded that we all make mistakes. You can carry this one step further and talk about the idea that we all expect to make mistakes nearly every day, and we all have to deal with imperfect situations every day. Our goal is to find a way to deal with them and not get bent out of shape when these things happen.

Some questions to ask include:

1. What exciting thing would you do if you were not afraid of making a mistake?

2. What part of your body begins to hurt when you feel afraid?

3. What words do you think of when you feel afraid?

4. What thoughts can you think to help you feel less afraid?

5. What do you like to have "perfect"?

6. Why is Pearla feeling so happy to go work in the bakery?

7. When Pearla sees that her cookies and cupcakes are imperfect, how does she feel?

8. How would you feel if something you made came out imperfect?

9. What does Pearla wish would happen in the bakery to make everything perfect again?

10. When does Pearla start to see that her cookies and cupcakes are perfect just the way they are?

11. Why do Mrs. Peggyopal and her daughter make Pearla feel sad? When has someone made you feel sad?

12. When the Peggyopals leave, who or what makes Pearla feel happy again?

13. Are square cookies and triangle cupcakes better than perfect round cookies and perfect tall cupcakes with wiggly white cream?

14. Did Pearla have a perfect day?

15. When have you had a perfect day?

Afterword

In my years of clinical practice as a cognitive behavioral psychologist specializing in anxiety disorders, there is a refrain that I find myself repeating: "I don't want you to be perfect" is a phrase that literally passes through my lips with almost every adult and child with whom I work.

The need to "be perfect," particularly for people with anxiety, is an all-encompassing drive. It is a goal that can never be achieved, thus leading to intense anxiety and feelings of hopelessness, helplessness, and negative self-worth. Alternately, learning how to "be imperfect," accepting and even embracing one's limitations, can reduce stress and be incredibly liberating.

In *Pearla and her Unpredictably Perfect Day*, Ms. Lieberman has captured the essence of this struggle to be perfect and the ability to use cognitive processes to control and triumph over fear and change behavior. Although written as a children's book, *Pearla* can be appreciated and used as a tool of change by children and adults alike.

Ms. Lieberman's background as a speech-language pathologist lends this book a unique perspective. The combination of emotional literacy and awareness and cognitive restructuring give the reader the skills he or she will need to begin the healthy journey toward imperfection.

Dr. Felice A. Tager,
Assistant Clinical Professor of
Medical Psychology in Psychiatry,
Columbia University Medical Center